SCREAMMATES™

MONSTER JAM

BY

KIERAN FLYNN

INTERIOR ILLUSTRATIONS BY
JASON VEGA

AN
APPLE
PAPERBACK

SCHOLASTIC INC.
New York Toronto London Auckland Sydney

For Heidi and all her little friends

ISBN 0-590-09896-9

Produced by Daniel Weiss Associates, Inc.
33 West 17th Street, New York, NY 10011

12 11 10 9 8 7 6 5 4 3 2 1   8 9/9 0 1 2/0

Printed in the U.S.A.   40

First Scholastic printing, March 1998

CHAPTER
ONE

"Boo-yah!"

That's what number 14 kept screaming every time he blocked my shot.

"Boo-yah, girl! This ain't no munchkin league, Shorty!"

That's what every player was screaming whenever I touched the basketball.

"Yo! Check it out! Shorty's got the ball again! Shoot it, Shorty! Go ahead and shoot!"

So what did I do? I kept shooting the ball. You know, when someone dares you to shoot, you have to shoot. But every time I took a shot . . . *Boo-yah!* It kept getting blocked! My teammates were getting angry.

My name, by the way, is *not* Shorty. It's Sarah Bardin, and I play point guard for the Marshall Tigers. We were playing the Thomas Jefferson Airplanes, one of the best schools around. We had lost a big lead and it was all my fault. I was pathetic out there. You know why? Because I'm a total dwarf.

Sarah Bardin. Fifth-grade dwarf.

I swear, I haven't grown since the second grade. Not one inch. All my teammates are at least a head taller than me. And they let me know it, too.

"Hey, dwarf!" yelled Wendy Stewart, one of the forwards on my team. "Don't you shoot that ball again! You shoot that ball again and I'm gonna pound your munchkin head into the floor!"

I felt my heart go into my throat and my teeth clench up. I hated Wendy Stewart. She was totally evil. She made fun of me every chance she got.

I knew I had to do something. I had to show her I could get the job done.

I had the ball at the top of the key. I faked left and drove straight to the hoop. Go up strong, I told myself. Got to go up strong! I leaped into the air and shot up the ball for a layup. I was going to do it this time!

Then I saw something out of the corner of my eye. It looked like a giant . . . hand.

"Boo-yaaah!" screamed number 14 as he swiped

my shot back down to the ground. He had blocked my shot *again*. One of the Jefferson Airplanes grabbed the ball, ran it downcourt, and scored.

"Time-out!" screamed Coach Jenkins. She did not look very happy.

My team walked back to the bench glaring at me. Wendy looked like she was going to bite my head off.

She bumped me to the side on her way to the bench. This sent me flying into a folding chair that I knocked down.

"What was that?" Coach Jenkins asked.

I saw the look on Wendy's face. I knew I'd better keep my mouth shut or I might get more than just a bump.

"Nothing," I said. "I'm fine."

But I wasn't fine. I was the dwarf who was losing us the game. The whole team hated me.

"All right, look," Coach Jenkins said. "There are ten seconds left on the clock. We can still win this one. We just need to play smart and get a good shot."

"Hey, Coach," said Wendy. "Just don't give the ball to the munchkin again."

"Yeah," said Jamal Wallace. "Let her go play in Munchkinland or something."

The whole team laughed. My stomach was trembling. My throat was tight. I could feel tears coming to my eyes, but I wasn't going to let them see me cry.

"Why don't you shut up, Jamal!" yelled Jeff Green. Jeff is my best friend and the starting center for the Tigers. He's always sticking up for me.

"Tell the little Smurf to find another sport," Wendy said. "How about hockey? She could be the puck!"

The team laughed again. Don't cry, I kept telling myself. Just don't cry.

"Shut up!" Jeff yelled.

"That's enough!" Coach Jenkins interrupted. "I don't want to hear any more of that kind of talk! We need to stick together! Now, we just need a good play here. We need a smart shot—"

"Coach!" Wendy interrupted. "Just get me the ball. If you get me the ball, I'll score. Just give me the ball!"

Coach Jenkins was silent for a second. Then she turned to me.

"Sarah," she said. "You're going to get the ball at half-court. Wendy's going to be under the basket. The second you get the ball, I want you to pass it inside to Wendy. Do you understand? Just pass it to Wendy."

"Yeah." I nodded. "I got it." I was still trying not to cry. Even Coach Jenkins didn't trust me with the ball. It was totally embarrassing. The whole team was against me. Except Jeff. Jeff was still trying to be a friend.

"It's cool," he said. "You can handle it, Sarah. One quick pass and you've got the assist. We're still in this. Just stay cool."

They blew the whistle and it was time to play. I was freaking out. I could feel my hands shaking. I tried to get myself together. You can do this, Sarah. You're not a munchkin, Sarah. Just one pass. One quick pass inside.

Jamal passed the ball in and I looked for Wendy inside. Everyone was crowding under the hoop. I had to spot her fast!

I could hear her yelling.

"Come on, dwarf! Where's the pass? Right here!"

All of a sudden, I saw two of the Jefferson Airplane uniforms running at me. They double-teamed me! And they were huge! I couldn't see a thing! I couldn't see past them at all! They had their hands up and they were waving their arms. It was like I was in the woods and they were these two huge trees!

I could still hear Wendy.

"Hey, dwarf! I'm open! *Where's the pass?*"

I could hear her all right. I just couldn't *see* her. I couldn't see *anything* over these guys.

Jamal was closer to me, but I couldn't see him, either!

"Come on, Shorty!" he was yelling. "I'm right here! Let go of the ball!"

But I couldn't see anything! And I couldn't move! The giants were swallowing me up with their double-team!

The last few seconds were a complete blur. I started sinking down to my knees like the dwarf I was. The whole team was screaming at me. Next thing I knew, the buzzer sounded.

The game was over. I had lost the game.

The Airplanes started celebrating their win, whooping and cheering. The Tigers walked off the court very slowly. I was still on my knees in the middle of the court, grasping the ball.

"Nice game," said Jamal sarcastically. "You really came through for us."

"Thanks a lot," I heard someone else say. I don't know who—I was keeping my head down. I didn't want to look at anyone.

"Hey, Bardin. I hear there's a game of Nerf

basketball down at the nursery school. Maybe you could handle that one."

I still had my head down when I felt someone's hands pick me up by the shoulders. I looked up. It was Wendy.

"You listen to me, dwarf," she said. "I don't want to see you anywhere near me in school tomorrow. If you see me coming down the stairs or down the hall, you better turn and run. Because if I run into you in school tomorrow, you know what I'm gonna do? I'm gonna drag you to my locker. Stuff your little dwarf body inside, lock the door, and forget the combination."

"Leave her alone!" yelled Jeff. He was now standing next to Wendy. "Let go of her right now."

"I was just leaving," said Wendy as she dropped me back on the floor and left the gym.

"Hey. Are you okay?" Jeff asked.

I couldn't take any more. I could feel myself starting to cry. I had to be alone. I had to get away.

I ran out of the gym, down the hallway, and into the stairwell. Then I just kept running down the stairs. Down and down. I didn't even know where I was going.

CHAPTER
TWO

I found a place to sit down and cry. And, man, did I cry. I was so upset. I buried my head in my hands.

"It's not fair!" I screamed. *"It's not fair!"*

My voice started echoing all around:

It's not faaair . . . not faaair . . . not faaair . . .

I felt something on my knee. Something ticklish. I picked up my head to look—

"Aaaahhhhh!"

Rat! There was a rat on my knee! It let out a high-pitched squeak and I shook my leg like crazy until it went flying off my leg and scurrying under a pipe.

My scream made another loud echo: *Aaaahhhhh . . . aaaahhhhh . . . aaaahhhhh . . .*

That's when I realized where I was.

I must have run down to the school basement, or maybe even the subbasement. I had never been here before. It was totally dark. And it was way too deserted. I could hear the water dripping from all the rusty pipes and the rats scurrying in and out of all the dark empty rooms. Was anyone *ever* down here? It didn't seem like it.

It was just me. Just the dwarf and a bunch of rats. I started to cry again.

That's when I heard a voice.

"Vhat's not fair, leetle girl?" asked the high-pitched voice. It was a weird-sounding voice with a weird accent.

"Who's there?" I called.

"Eet ees me," the high-pitched voice replied.

"Where are you?" I asked.

The voice didn't answer. Instead, all I heard was a little squeak. One little squeak . . . and then another. And then another.

First the squeaks were little. But as they got closer . . . they got a lot louder. And a lot *bigger.* Something was making *giant* squeaks. And that something was getting closer! The giant squeaks were echoing all over the basement!

10

Squeeeeak, squeak-squeak, squeeeeak, squeeeeeak!

I started backing myself farther and farther into a corner of the disgusting room.

Squeak-squeak, squeeeeeeak, squeak-squeeeeak!

"Who's there?" I screamed.

SQUEEEEEEEEEEEEEAK!

I shut my eyes and screamed, "*Aaaahhhh!*"

Then the voice said, "Vhat? Vhat? Vhy all de crying and screaming?"

I opened my eyes. It was a little old woman. She was pushing a mop and bucket on wheels. Very squeaky wheels.

"You scared me!" I said.

"Vhat's scary about a leetle old woman weeth a mop?" she asked.

"I thought you were a—Oh, never mind." I collapsed back down on the floor. "This is the worst day of my life!"

"Vhat's de matter, leetle girl? I hear you screaming, 'Eet's not faaair. Eet's not faaair!' You pretty loud for a leetle girl. Vhat's so unfair dat you scream about? And vhat you doing down here? Dees ees no place for a leetle girl—"

"*Stop it!*" I screamed. "Stop calling me a little girl! I'm not *that* little! I'm . . . I'm . . . ooooh!"

I started thinking about the game and Wendy and I started to cry again.

"Oh, boy," the old woman said. "Such a sensitive leetle girl."

"You want to know what's the matter?" I said. "Look at me! I'm not just a 'leetle' girl—I'm a *dwarf*! I'm a stupid little dwarf and that's why I *stink* at basketball! The whole team hates me. They don't want me to play. And it's because they're all *taller* than me. The whole fifth *grade* is taller than me! I can't stand it anymore. All I want is to be *tall*! Is that so much to ask?"

"Oh, leetle girl—"

"Stop calling me that!" I interrupted.

"Sorry, sorry," said the old woman. "I don't vant you to be so upset!"

The old woman walked over and sat next to me. "Eet's not so bad to be small. Look at me! I'm very small. But very happy. Look at all my leetle friends here. You hear them? 'Squeak, squeak!' So cute, eh?"

Her best friends were *rats*? She was weirder than I thought.

"My leetle friends can do many theengs no one else can do, you see? They very fast. They can find leetle holes. Get through theengs like no one else, eh? You understand? I bet you can do theengs on basketball court, theengs de tall ones can't do, eh? Find de holes! Use de speed!"

"It doesn't matter," I told her. "I'm always going to be too small. I'm sick of it! I *need* to be taller. I want to be taller than *all of them*!"

"Yes," she said. "But you not using enough of vhat you *do* have—"

"You're not listening to me!" I yelled. I was so fed up. "I don't *want* what I have! I want to be huge! I don't want to be small like some tiny *rat*!"

Angry squeaks and squeals started coming from behind the walls and inside all the pipes. Even under the ground.

"*Vhat's wrong weeth being like a rat?*" the old woman shrieked. I started to feel a little uneasy.

"Uhhh . . . nothing," I said. My voice was a little shaky. "I mean . . . rats are . . . cool."

"You theenk you have to be so tall, eh?" she asked angrily. "You theenk dat's de only way you *ever* going to be happy?"

"Yeah, but I didn't mean—"

"No one vants to be leetle like a dirty leetle *rat*, eh?"

"I'm sorry—" I tried to apologize, but it was no use.

"You hear that, my leetle friends?" the old woman shouted. "She doesn't vant to be like a *rat*. She vants to be *taaaall. Ooooooh*."

The rats' squeals were getting out of control!

"All I meant was—"

"I know vhat you meant!" she screamed. *"Okaaaaay,"* she announced slowly. "You vant to be tall? We gonna make you *tall*. We gonna see how you like it!"

"What are you talking about?" I asked. I was slowly getting up, moving back toward the stairway.

"I'm talking about magic! Vhat you theenk I'm talking about?" she squealed.

My legs were starting to shake. I had to get out of there.

"Look," I said. "I'm sorry if I, uh . . . I mean . . . this is your home, I guess . . . and *I* should really be getting back to *my* home, so I'm sorry if—"

"Silence!" she demanded. "You don't theenk we have the power? If I say we have the power, we have the power. You understand? *Come here, leetle girl. We gonna grant you your weesh!"*

14

"I really have to go now!" I screamed back at her. "It was really nice meeting you!"

I turned to run, but the old woman jumped up and grabbed my arms.

The only thing was, her hands didn't feel like they were *hands* anymore. They felt more like little . . . *claws*!

"*Heeeeelp meeeee!*" I screamed. "*Somebody help meeeee!*"

CHAPTER
THREE

Rats started scurrying out from every room in the basement. They were falling out of pipes, squeezing out of holes. Soon the entire floor was *covered* with squealing rats!

The old woman's claws were digging into my arms.

"Please!" I begged. "Let me go!"

"But we're going to help you," she whispered. *"We're going to make you nice and tall for de basketball! Hee-hee-hee-hee-heeeee."*

Her laugh sounded just like the rats' squeals. They squealed along with her.

Eee-hee-hee! Eee-hee-hee-hee-heeeee!

"Silence!" she yelled. There was complete

silence in the room. The only things I could hear were my teeth chattering.

"P-P-Please," I stammered. "D-D-Don't hurt me."

"I told you!" she insisted. "I'm going to *help* you. . . . Let the spell begin!"

She stamped her foot on the wet, rat-covered floor and the lights started flickering on and off. The rats started climbing all over each other. The old woman's grip on my arms got even tighter.

"Ow!" I screamed. But it was no use. She had started some kind of crazy mumbling. She was mumbling and squeaking. The rats were squeaking back. I didn't know what she was saying. But then she started chanting about me!

"De girl believes she ees too small,
We cast dis spell to make her tall!
Now nothing will be as eet seems,
Dis girl will live all her hoop dreams!"

The squeals began to grow. The rats were scurrying over my shoes! Even crawling on my legs!

"Now look to me!" she screamed. "Look deep into my eyes. *Look behind my eyes!*"

She grabbed my head and forced me to look up

at her. Her face was flashing in the flickering lights. But I could still make out her eyes . . . and they were totally black! Just two little black eyeballs!

"Who ees de favorite player?" she demanded.

"*Please*," I begged, "just let me—"

She shook my whole body. She was getting stronger! She brought her face closer and stared at me with her black eyes. I felt something start to slither around my legs. It was coming from behind the old woman . . . *a tail*!

"Who ees de favorite player? *Tell me now!*"

"Shaquille!" I cried. "Shaquille O'Neal!"

"Vhat ees his number?" she demanded.

"His number?"

"Yes! De number on de jersey! Vhat ees de number?"

Her tail was pulling tighter and tighter around my legs!

"It's thirty-four! His number is thirty-four! Let me go!" I yelled. But she had already started chanting again.

"De leetle girl has struck a deal
Weeth de number of Shakweel O'Neel.
Eef she decides her life's too tough
Thirty-four stuffs make her tall enough!
Squeeeeeak-squeak-squeeeeeak!"

The lights were flashing faster and faster. A huge wind started howling through the room. The wind was blowing the little rats smack against the cold wall. They were squealing and scurrying, trying to escape its force. The old woman was still holding me steady. She let out one last, huge squeal and I saw her black eyes and her two giant rat teeth coming toward my face!

And then it was over. The old woman looked normal again.

The wind died down and she let go of my arms and my legs. I just stood there in shock.

"Eet ees done," she said. "De magic is done . . . de rest ees up to you, you understand? Your choice. Eef you vant dis magic, you must slahm-dunk de basketball *thirty-four times*. Then you *grow*. Then—*squeeeeeak*—we see just how much—*squeeeeeak*—de leetle girl likes being tall! *Hee-hee-hee-hee-squeeeeeak!*"

The rats all started squealing like they were laughing, too.

"Well, go on!" she cried, laughing. "Get going! *Hee-hee-hee!* Get out there and slahm, slahm, slahm! *Hee-hee-hee-hee-squeeeeeak!* But I tell you right now—you'll be back! You'll be *baaaaack!* *Hee-hee-hee-hee. Squeak-squeak-squeeeeeak!*"

CHAPTER FOUR

I don't even remember walking home. I just kept hearing the squeals over and over in my head. *Squeak-squeak-squeak!* Ugh! And the old woman's rat face! Yuck! It was horrible. I must have looked like a total zombie walking down the street to my house. When I finally got home, Jeff was waiting for me, shooting baskets in my driveway.

"Where have you been?" he asked. "I couldn't find you after the game. Are you all right? You're as white as a mouse."

"A *what*? A *what*?" I cried.

"Hey, hey, calm down. It's just an expression!" he said.

"I'm sorry," I said. "I'm just a little upset."

I wanted to tell Jeff about what had happened, but I knew he wouldn't believe me. He'd think I'd completely flipped my lid. I wasn't so sure I hadn't.

"It was a tough loss," Jeff said. "But it wasn't all your fault. You should have gotten more help. Who knew they were gonna double-team you?"

"Huh?" I asked.

"The game. Remember? The game we just played *today*? Hello? Is anybody there?"

I was still pretty weirded out. I had to try to get myself together.

"Oh, yeah," I finally answered. "Today's game. I remember."

"Sarah," Jeff said, looking pretty concerned. "What is wrong with you?"

I had to snap out of it. Get it together, Sarah. You can't tell him.

"I'm okay, Jeff. Really. I'm okay now."

"You're sure?" he asked.

"Yes," I said, rubbing my eyes and taking a deep breath. "I'm sure."

"Okay," he said. He seemed pretty convinced. "You wanna play a little one-on-one?"

I thought about it for a second and decided that was just what I needed to calm down. A little game of round ball. Driveway hoops with Jeff always made me feel better.

"Yeah. That sounds good," I told him. "That sounds good."

"Cool," he said, smiling. "Take it out."

He tossed me the ball and we started to play. I was a little shaky at first, but once I got focused on just playing ball, I started to get into my rhythm.

Jeff's a lot taller than me, but once I get my ball control going, I can always beat him off the dribble. I was going between the legs, behind the back. I've even got my own sort of crossover dribble. Well, sort of. Anyway, once I really calmed down, Jeff was getting beaten *bad*.

"Hey, Sarah," he said, standing still just a little too long.

"Yeah?" I asked as I faked right and went left for the layup.

"How come you never play like this in the games? Or even in practice?"

"Like what?" I asked as I did a quick little spin to the hoop.

"Like *that*," he answered, laughing. "You're so quick. You've got incredible ball control. You've got the quickest first step of anyone I know. How come you only play that way in the driveway?"

"Oh, *that*," I said, trying not to feel embarrassed. "Well, when Wendy's around making jokes and . . . you know, the rest of the team joins in . . . I just get . . . nervous. I just can't be *me*. It's like, when they call me a dwarf and stuff, then that's what I become. You know what I mean?"

"That sounds dumb to me," Jeff said.

"Yeah, I guess," I said. "Because they don't get to see me do stuff like this."

I put on an all-out dribbling display for Jeff. I was doing a pretty good Harlem Globetrotters imitation. We were both having a good laugh and I was actually starting to feel better—until I heard Wendy's voice.

"Hey, dwarf! You practicing for *team mascot*?"

Wendy's house is down the road from mine. She must have been walking home. The second I heard her voice, I lost my dribble. The ball bounced up and hit me in the chin. Then it rolled into the yard. Wendy started laughing.

"Nice one!" she yelled.

"Why don't you get out of here, Wendy!" Jeff yelled back.

"I'm going!" she said. "I just wanted to tell the dwarf something!"

"What do you want?" I asked, rubbing my chin.

"I just wanted you to know that a few of the kids and I went to talk to Coach after the game. We told her that we didn't think you should be on the team. We've still got a shot at the championship and we don't want you to mess it up! See ya later, dwarf!"

My teeth clenched up and so did my fists. I think my whole body clenched up. I was so angry, I thought my head would explode.

"I . . . hate . . . Wendy . . . Stewart."

"It's okay," Jeff said, trying to calm me down. "Don't freak out. I'm sure Coach didn't listen to 'em."

But I wasn't listening to Jeff. That was it. I'd had enough. Who was I kidding? The dwarf was never going to win any games. Now the dwarf wasn't even going to be on the team!

The nightmare in the basement was all coming back to me. Was any of it real? Was I crazy? A psycho rat woman? Magic? I had to find out. I had to see if it was all *real*!

"Jeff," I said through clenched teeth. "Have you ever heard of a fifth-grader who could slam-dunk?"

"No," he replied.

"Me neither," I said. "There's a trampoline in the backyard and a mattress in the garage. I'm gonna need your help."

CHAPTER
FIVE

Jeff helped me move the trampoline onto the driveway, right in front of the basket. That was for the jump to the hoop. Then we put the mattress right under the basket. That was for coming down.

"I really don't think this is a good idea," Jeff kept saying. "You shouldn't let Wendy get to you like this."

"You don't have to help if you don't want to," I told him.

We got everything into place.

"Okay," I said. "Do you want to test it or should I?"

"Let me test it first," Jeff said. "I'm taller."

"Not for long," I said under my breath.

"What?" he asked.

"Nothing," I said. "You go ahead and test it. *Then it's my turn.*"

Jeff was looking at me like I was some kind of maniac. I kind of felt like I *was* one.

Jeff grabbed the ball and backed up on the driveway. He took a running start and jumped onto the trampoline. He went flying up, but he missed the hoop completely! He smashed into the garage door.

"Ugh!" he moaned.

My mom called from the kitchen window.

"Honey! What's going on out there?"

"Nothing!" I called back. "Jeff and I are just playing a little ball!"

"Okay," she said, sounding a little worried. "Just be careful!"

"We will!" I told her. "Give me the ball," I told Jeff.

"Are you nuts?" he replied. "Didn't you see what just happened to me? You'll break your neck!"

"*Just give me the ball!*" I screamed.

"Man, what's wrong with you today? It was just one game."

"It's not one game, Jeff! It's my whole life! My life as a *dwarf*! And I've had it! I don't care

27

what happens. I'm gonna dunk this ball thirty-four times if it takes all night!"

"*Thirty-four times?*" he blurted in shock.

"That's right! Now give me the ball!" I demanded.

"Fine!" he yelled back. "But you're on your own! I don't know what happened to you today, but hopefully you'll be normal tomorrow. *If* you don't break your neck tonight. You're nuts! See ya tomorrow!"

Jeff grabbed his bag and ran down the road, shaking his head. Fine, I thought. I didn't need his help. It was all up to me now. Thirty-four stuffs would make me tall enough!

I backed up on the driveway and started running. I hit the trampoline and went flying. *Up, up . . .*

Right into the garage door.

Oompf!

That's okay, I told myself. You'll get it. Just keep practicing.

The misses went on for a while. I was collecting bruises all over my shoulders. My hands were getting scraped up, too. But I didn't care how much my body ached. Keep going, I told myself.

On my fifteenth try, I slammed one! And, ooh, what a feeling!

"*Boo-yah!*" I screamed. "In your face!"

That's one down! Just thirty-three to go. . . .

I have no idea how long I was out there, but I really started to get the timing right. I was slamming them home!

Right around dunk number twenty-five, it started to rain. It started as a light drizzle.

But the closer I got to thirty-four, the heavier the rain got. I was wiping the water out of my eyes, wiping the water off the ball, but I wouldn't stop. I couldn't stop now!

Slam!

"Thirty-one!" I screamed. I picked myself up, grabbed the ball, and headed back to the front of the driveway.

Slam!

"Thirty-two!"

Now it was pouring rain. The sky was completely black and the wind was blowing the leaves off the trees! My hair was blowing straight back from my head. I had to squint to see the basket and keep the pouring rain out of my eyes!

"*Sarah Bardin!*" my mom yelled from the kitchen window. "You get in here right now! What are you doing out there in this rain? *Right now, young lady!*"

Can't stop now, I told myself. Got to finish this.

"I'm coming!" I called to her.

Slam!

"Thirty-three!"

"I said right now!" my mom screamed.

One more! Just one more! I backed up and started running. I hit the trampoline and leaped into the air.

The wind was so hard that it was throwing me at the hoop!

It was coming too fast! My head was on a collision course with the rim!

You can do this, Sarah. Arms out! Arms out!

Slam!

"Thirty-four!" I hollered.

The thunder pounded my eardrums! And then I heard . . .

Squeaking. Squeaking and squealing.

Hee-hee-hee-hee. Squeeeeak-squeeeeeeak!

I looked around, but it was just me. Just me lying flat on a mattress in my driveway, the rain pouring down on my head.

And I was still a dwarf.

How stupid could I be? Of *course* I was still a dwarf.

One wet, stupid, depressed dwarf.

My mother walked outside and dragged me back into the house.

CHAPTER
SIX

Somehow I managed to drag myself to practice the next day. I don't know how I did it. I was afraid to show my face. Coach Jenkins was probably going to throw me off the team. And the second I walked in . . .

"Well, look who's here!" Wendy shouted. "Hey! Did someone here order shrimp?"

Everyone laughed.

"Don't even bother getting changed," said Jamal. "No one's gonna pass it to you, peewee."

They laughed again.

"I think you should just *go home*," said Wendy.

I felt sick to my stomach. How much more of this could I take? Maybe Wendy was right.

Maybe I just should have gone home. Nothing was ever going to change. The thought made me feel even sicker.

Jeff came up to me and gave me a pat on the back.

"Are you okay?" he asked. "You were totally nuts yesterday."

"I'm sorry about that," I said. "Let's just forget yesterday, okay? The whole thing was a big waste of time. Just pretend it never happened. I'm gonna go get changed."

What's the point? I thought, heading for the locker room. Wendy's right. I should just go home now. What am I even here for?

I went to my locker and changed into my sweats.

At least, I *thought* they were my sweats.

I must have grabbed someone else's by mistake. My shorts always hang over my knees.

But these shorts were hanging *above* my knees.

I checked the name tag. They were definitely my shorts.

My jersey was shorter on me, too.

No way.

Something was *definitely* weird.

I ran back onto the court for drills.

We lined up to shoot layups. The weird thing

33

was, standing in line with my teammates . . . they had all grown a little shorter! Either that, or maybe—just *maybe*—*I* had grown a little *taller.*

I got my bounce pass and went up for the layup. Was I seeing things or was the basket a little closer?

Please don't let me be imagining this!

We started to play a game, but it was just like Jamal said. No one would pass me the ball. It was like he and Wendy had told the team not to pass it to me. I was getting really frustrated. But I just kept my mouth shut and ran back and forth.

Jeff finally saw me open and gave me a pass. Just my luck. Wendy jumped out to cover me.

"Come on, dwarf! *Shoot it*," she said, mocking me. "I think there's a bug on the court! Maybe I should step on it! Come on, munchkin, give it up! Don't forget, *Coach is watching.*"

Coach *is* watching, I thought. I've got to do *something*. I don't want to get thrown off this team!

I looked Wendy in the eye and started my move. I faked left, then right, then went behind the back and right up.

Wendy jumped up with me.

I kept my eye on the rim and released the ball.

Her hand was up in my face and it was

coming toward the ball! *But I shot it* over *her outstretched hand!*

Swish!

"Yes!" screamed Jeff.

"Yes!" I screamed.

"Great shot, Sarah!" yelled Coach Jenkins from the sideline. "That showed some real confidence!"

Wendy was standing there stunned.

"What's the big deal?" she said. "One lucky shot? So what? She's still a *dwarf!*"

"Yeah," said Jamal, laughing. "But that dwarf just made you look *real bad.* Ha-ha-ha-haaaah!"

"Shut up!" screamed Wendy.

"It's real!" I screamed. "I can't believe it! It's really real! *The magic is real!*"

"What are you, an NBA commercial?" Wendy yelled. "It was *just one shot!*"

But I wasn't listening. I was too excited! I was only thinking one thing!

Look out, world! Sarah Bardin is growing!

CHAPTER
SEVEN

I woke up the next morning and jumped out of bed. I ran over to my bookshelf, where I'd been measuring myself ever since I could stand. The last mark was from third grade. I'd stayed that height for *two years*. But I made my first new mark after last night's practice. I grew *two inches* yesterday.

I grabbed my ruler and stood next to the bookshelf. I grew another *four inches* overnight. That made *six inches in less than twenty-four hours*!

I spent the next twenty minutes just staring at myself in the mirror. This was so cool.

"Sarah!" my mom called from downstairs. "You're going to be late for school!"

"Sorry!" I called back. "I'm getting ready!"

I tried to get dressed for school, but my jeans didn't fit me anymore! This was *so cool*! I found a big pair of sweatshorts and a long shirt and got ready to go.

I ran downstairs, right past my parents. I had to meet Jeff to walk to school. I grabbed a piece of toast and flew out the door. Jeff was waiting outside.

"Hey!" I said.

"Hey," he said. Then he just stared at me.

"What?" I asked.

"Huh?" he grunted.

"What are you staring at?"

"Uhhh . . ." Jeff had a puzzled expression on his face. "Are you, like . . . wearing high heels or something?"

"No," I said, smiling. "Why?"

"It just seems like . . . you're a lot . . . taller."

"Yeah," I said. "I think I'm finally getting my growth spurt."

"Huh. That was . . . way fast. Your growth spurt."

"I *know*." I giggled. "I've just been eating *a lot* of Wheaties. And I think it's finally paying off!"

"Huh," he said. "Wow . . . I guess so!" he

37

said finally, laughing along with me. "Well, I hope you ate enough Wheaties for the game tonight. You know we're playing the Lincoln Logs."

The Abraham Lincoln Logs. They were a great team. They were a *tall* team.

"Yeah, I know," I told him. "I'm ready."

CHAPTER
EIGHT

"What are you, some kind of alien or something?" Wendy Stewart asked, her eyebrows all twisted and her mouth puckered up. She was staring at me.

"I'm not an alien," I said calmly. "I'm just growing up."

That was no lie. I *was* growing up. *Way* up. We were changing for the game against the Lincoln Logs and I had already grown a full *foot*.

"Nobody grows a *foot* in a *day*," Wendy snorted.

"Nobody but *me*," I told her, smiling.

"Alien!" she barked.

I looked right into her eyes. I could do that now.

"I'm no alien," I told her. *"Just pass me the ball."*

"In your *dreams*, dwarf . . . or . . . alien . . . or whatever you are! You're not gonna get a pass from me!"

"What's the matter, Wendy? Afraid I might just *show you up again*?"

Wendy's face turned beet red. But she had nothing to say. I had finally shut her up. She just slammed her locker and stormed off. I had a huge grin on my face. I was feeling good. I was feeling *very* good.

Until I heard it again.

The squeaking.

Squeak-squeak-squeeeeeak. Hee-hee-hee-heeeee!

My whole body started to feel funny. Kind of like it was tingling. You know how people say that something made their skin crawl? That's kind of how I felt. Like my skin was crawling. The only thing was . . . when I looked down at my arms and legs . . .

My skin *was* crawling!

Something was scurrying all around *under my skin*!

And I could actually see my limbs stretching! My arms and legs were squeaking with every

41

little stretch as the little lumps were scurrying all over my body!

Squeeeeeak-squeak-squeak-squeeeeeak!

I started flashing back to the basement. Rats everywhere, falling in batches out of the pipes! Crawling on my legs!

"*Ahhhhh!*" I screamed.

Next thing I knew the crawling and stretching had stopped. I looked up and saw that I was eye level with the top shelf of my locker!

Stay calm, Sarah. It's okay, I told myself. Tall is good. Don't get scared. It's just going to make you better. Now let's go out there and whip those Lincoln Logs!

That's exactly what I did, too. I kicked the Lincoln Logs' butts. I mean, I was all over the court. I was penetrating at will. No one could stop me. If someone stopped my move, I just went straight up for the shot! Right over all their heads!

Swish!

The crowd was going crazy! They loved me!

I was even posting up inside. One quick move and a turnaround jumper.

Swish! Nothing but net.

It was just like Shaq! I was playing ball like Shaq!

Wendy did not look psyched. She kept frowning and giving me mean looks. But she kept her mouth shut. And the rest of the team was giving me high fives.

Jeff was hooting and hollering for me. He kept feeding me the ball.

"Go on, Sarah!" he shouted. "Right inside! Right inside!"

I made a sweet little spin toward the hoop, followed by a reverse layup.

"Yes!" Jeff screamed.

Even Jamal was giving me high fives!

"That was *sweet*, Bardin!" he yelled. "You are most definitely the *truth*! Wooooo!"

We came out of one time-out and Wendy started talking to the rest of the team.

"Okay, guys," she said. "You better start passing the ball to me, 'cause you know the alien here is gonna start messing up any second."

That's when Jamal actually defended me.

"Shut up, Wendy," he shouted. "Bardin's gonna get us to the championship! Right, Bardin?"

"That's the *truth*!" I told him.

We won the game. And we won every game after that.

I was growing a little bit *every day*.

And we were unstoppable! The crowd was loving me! They even gave me a nickname: "Lady Shaq."

Every time I got the ball, the crowd would start chanting.

"Lady Shaq! Lady Shaq! Lady Shaq!"

It all came down to a rematch against the Jefferson Airplanes. If we could beat the Airplanes, we would be in the championship.

And guess who was blocking all the shots this time?

"Boo-yah!" I screamed as I blocked number 14's shot.

That's what I'd been screaming the whole game.

"Boo-yah! Come on, Shorty! You can do better than that!"

The Airplanes all looked like dwarves to me.

We were embarrassing them! We were destroying them!

And in the final seconds of the game, they even tried to double-team me! They didn't just double-team me! They *triple-teamed* me! I mean, *come on*!

It must have been a pretty funny image. I just stood there, holding the ball above my head, while these poor kids were leaping up and down like little dogs, trying to swat the ball away from me.

The crowd was laughing and chanting my nickname.

"Lady Shaq! Lady Shaq! Lady Shaq!"

I waited until Jeff was open. I threw a quick bullet pass to him in the lane. He scored at the final buzzer.

The crowd went nuts! We had made it to the championship! We were going to play the Washington Monuments for the championship! Everything was absolutely perfect! My life was perfect.

Until I woke up the next morning.

CHAPTER

NINE

"What's that? Who's there?"

Something had jolted me awake. It was a sound! The most hideous, totally ear-shattering sound.

I was dreaming about a car screeching to a halt, or . . . maybe it was someone scratching her nails down a chalkboard. But it was like it went on forever!

Like I had been hearing it all night!

The most awful sort of . . . *squeaking*.

Oh, no.

Hee-hee-hee-hee-squeak-squeak-hee-hee-hee-heeeee!

"Who's there?" I screamed. "Where are

you? I know you're there! Stay away from me!"

I started flailing around in my bed, punching at the sheets and the pillow. I knew they were there! I could hear them. I could *feel* them!

I kept punching, but my punches were out of control! My arm flapped back and I hit myself in the face!

"Ow!" I screamed. How did that happen?

Then I looked at my arm.

It was huge.

No wonder I couldn't control it.

And if my arm was so huge, what about . . .

Oh, no.

I peered under the sheets at the rest of my body.

My legs stretched entirely off the bed. I couldn't even see my feet. They were down on the floor somewhere!

I jumped out of bed and stumbled over to my bookshelf.

It's not that bad, I told myself. Don't worry. The bigger the better, right?

I couldn't measure myself on my bookshelf.

I was *taller* than my bookshelf!

Okay, Sarah. Just stay calm. It's not as bad as you think. You're fine. No one will even notice the difference.

I went downstairs for breakfast.

When my mom saw me, she let out a huge gasp. She dropped the maple syrup on the floor.

My dad dropped his fork, and his glasses fell on top of his pancakes.

"What?" I asked them.

My parents just stared at me.

"Nothing," my mom said finally. "Er . . . have some pancakes?"

"Yes, thank you," I said. No one was talking to me.

"What, Dad?" I shouted. "What are you staring at?"

"Um . . . nothing," he said.

We kept eating until my little brother, Will, came down to the table. He's seven.

"Wow!" he shouted. "I'm living with a real live *giant*!"

"I am not a giant!" I screamed.

"Sweetheart," my mom said. "I know how happy you've been about your growing, but something is very wrong. This is not normal! I think we should take you to a doctor right away!"

"I don't need any doctor!" I yelled. "You don't know what you're talking about. I'm probably gonna make it to the WNBA! Look at me! I'm gonna be a professional basketball player! *I'm fine!*"

I scarfed down a stack of fifteen pancakes and guzzled the gallon of milk on the table. Then I stormed outside for practice.

Jeff was waiting for me in the driveway. I tapped him on the shoulder and he turned around.

"Ahhhhh!" he screamed.

"What?" I screamed back.

Jeff was looking up at me and his hands were sort of trembling.

"Oh . . . nothing," he said. "I'm just . . . happy to see you?"

We walked to practice and Jeff didn't say a word. He just kept looking up at me.

CHAPTER

TEN

When I walked into practice, everything stopped.

The team's mouths all dropped open. Balls stopped dribbling and went rolling toward the bleachers. Jamal spilled his Gatorade all over the court. There was total silence. Of course, the first person to speak . . . was Wendy.

"Looks like Lady Shaq had a 'Shaq attack'!" she snorted.

The kids laughed.

"Hey, Bardin!" she shouted. "How's the air up there?"

I could feel my face turning red.

"Hey! Chewbacca! I'm talking to you!"

The kids laughed again.

"I hear you, Wendy!" I shouted. "Why don't you just give me the ball and do your talking on the court!"

"You got it, Chewy! Here you go!"

She tossed me the ball and took a defensive stance.

"Let's go, Frankenstein!" She giggled. "Take your shot!"

There was no way I was going to let Wendy start in on me again. Not now! I'd embarrass her on the court. *That* would keep her quiet.

I faked left, then right, followed by a quick spin.

Or at least that's what I had planned to do.

Instead, my legs just got kind of tangled up. I lost the ball on my first dribble! It just went through my legs and off into the bleachers.

"Hey!" Wendy snorted. "Great shot, Chewy! Check it out, guys! The human jumbo pretzel! I'll take one with mustard!"

"Uh-oh-ho-ho-ha-ha-haaah!" Jamal laughed.

"*Give me the ball, Jamal!*" I demanded, thrusting my arm down at him.

He stopped laughing immediately.

"Yes, ma'am," he said, raising the ball up to me.

I turned back to Wendy.

"Look out, Wendy," I stated.

So the fancy moves were out. Fine! I was big enough to just charge toward the basket. Nothing was going to stand in my way! *Look out, Wendy! Here comes Lady Shaq!*

I ran at the basket.

But I couldn't run and dribble at the same time! The ball bounced right off my foot!

I tripped over my own legs.

"Woo!" Wendy hooted. "I don't think you get it, Chewy! You're supposed to dribble the ball *while* you run!"

The team laughed again.

"Bardin," Jamal said. "What's wrong with you? You should join the circus, 'cause you're, like, a major freak. We're talking major freak show!"

"I'm not a freak!" I yelled back. "You guys don't know what you're talking about! You're just jealous 'cause I'm going to the Women's NBA!"

"Yeah, right!" Wendy answered. "You can't even dribble! Look at you. You're an alien!"

"I am not an alien! I'm just *growing*!"

I was trying to be strong, but the truth was, I was getting scared. I went over to Jeff for some help.

"Jeff," I said. "What's going on? How come you're not backing me up with Wendy? Tell her I'm not an alien!"

Jeff wasn't saying anything. He just kept staring up at me.

"Jeff? What's going on? Say something!"

He was opening his mouth, but he wasn't talking!

"Jeff! Stop staring at me and *say something*!"

"Sarah," he said, sounding really serious. "You need to see a doctor. You're like . . . some kind of *mutant* or something."

I couldn't believe it. Jeff was my best friend in the whole world. And even he was calling me a mutant!

"I am not a mutant!" I yelled at him. "I'm just fine! *You're* the mutant! You're *all* mutants! You all look like a bunch of dwarves to me! You wanna see what I can do? I'll show you what I can do!"

I grabbed the ball and started galloping toward the hoop. No dribbling. I didn't need to dribble. I took two huge steps and I stuffed the ball into that hoop!

Slam!

Crash!

The whole backboard shattered. Glass came shattering down all over the court! The kids were running from the hoop screaming! Coach Jenkins came running onto the court.

She gave me the meanest look.

So did Wendy.

So did Jeff.

They were all staring at me.

"Stare all you want!" I yelled. "I'll see all you dwarves tomorrow at the championship game! I hope you all remember who *got* you to the championship game! *Have a nice day!*"

I turned around slowly and stomped off the court.

I hoped I sounded real brave and self-confident, because the fact was . . . I was really scared.

Jeff hated me. Coach Jenkins hated me. The team hated me. The whole *school* probably hated me because they'd have to replace the backboard by tomorrow.

But much worse than all of that?

The thing that was scaring me the most?

I was growing.

I was *still* growing!

And I was growing faster and faster.

CHAPTER
ELEVEN

It was the night of the big game. The game I'd wanted to get to all season! And I was hiding in the rest room.

It was happening again! It was happening all the time now! The horrible squeaking! The stretching!

Squeak-squeak-hee-hee-hee-hee-heeeee!

I never knew where it was going to happen!

I couldn't even fit into the stall without bending my head down and folding my arms.

I started to lean hard to my left. I looked down and my right leg was growing!

My skin was practically bubbling with little squeaky creatures! And the leg *stretched . . . and stretched*! Now the right leg was a foot longer than the left!

Then I heard her voice.

"How you like it now, leetle girl? Or should I say, beeg, beeg girl? Now you nice and tall, eh? Beeger than all the rest, eh? You happy? *Hee-hee-hee-hee-squeeeak!*"

"What have you done to me?" I screamed as my left leg *stretched* to match the right.

"Now," she squealed, "you really going to get it! *Hee-hee-heeeee!*"

There was a pounding at the bathroom door.

Was it her?

Pound! Pound! Pound!

In her most disgusting form?

Hee-hee-hee-hee-squeeeak!

"Go away!" I screeched.

Pound! Pound! Pound!

"Hey, Sarah!" Jeff screamed from the other side of the door. "Are you in there?"

It was Jeff. Just Jeff.

"Yeah!" I called back to him.

"Sarah," he said. "You've gotta come out of there. The game's starting. What are you doing in there?"

"Just go away, Jeff," I whined.

"Come on!" he called. Then he spoke a little

more quietly through the door. "Sarah . . . I'm really sorry about what I said yesterday. You're not a mutant."

Yeah right, I thought. He hasn't seen me today!

"And I'm sorry I didn't stick up for you," he continued. "I just got a little scared. But I'm not scared anymore. I mean, what's the difference whether you're two feet tall, or ten, or fifty, or whatever! I mean, we're still best friends, right? So you shouldn't be scared, either, because I'll be right there with you."

Jeff was right. I had to go out there and play. I had to!

I forced myself out of the stall and opened the bathroom door.

"Ahh!" Jeff screamed. "Uh . . . sorry. I'm just . . . excited for the game! You ready?" he asked.

"Yeah," I told him as I ducked under the bathroom doorway.

But I was lying.

I wasn't ready.

I was doomed.

When I walked onto the court, the crowd started going nuts!

But they weren't cheering.

They were screaming in shock.

I kept my head down and tried to take a few warm-up shots. All misses. I could hear the crowd freaking out on the sidelines. I suddenly wished I could be invisible.

"What is that?" they were screaming at Coach Jenkins. "Is this a joke?"

"What is she? Some kind of mutant or something?"

"You can't let that thing play basketball! It's not safe for the other children!"

"Send her back to the circus!"

Coach Jenkins tried to explain that I was a member of the team, but they were still yelling and complaining.

The game started and the first time I got the ball . . .

The whole gym started booing.

I tried to dribble to the hoop, but I tripped all over myself and coughed it up.

The boos got even louder.

The whole first half was just the crowd booing and screaming. At *me*.

Wendy walked over to me in a time-out.

"Do us all a favor, freak! Don't touch the ball again!"

I kept trying to move with the ball. I thought I could make my body play! But all my moves had the same result!

Total disaster!

"*Booooo!*" the crowd shouted.

It was awful! I couldn't play! They hated me! They didn't just hate me, they were *afraid* of me! Afraid I might step on the other kids or something!

"*Booooo!*" they shouted again. "Get out of the game! Get out of this gym! Go back to your own *planet*!"

I couldn't take it anymore. I couldn't take another minute of it! The booing! The screaming! The insults! I'd had *enough*. I smashed the ball down and stormed off the court.

The crowd cheered as I left the gym. I didn't care. I didn't care what they thought anymore. I only cared about one thing.

"Where are you going?" Jeff asked, grabbing my arm.

"I'll be back," I told him.

This whole thing had to stop!

I was going back to the basement.

CHAPTER
TWELVE

"*Where are you?*" I belted. "Come on, *rat woman*! I know you're down here!"

I could hear them all scurrying around the dark basement, laughing their little repulsive laugh.

Hee-hee-hee-hee-heeeee!

"Shut up!" I demanded. "I'm so sick of that sound! I'm so sick of this whole thing! *Where are you?*"

"Looking for me?" came a squeak from behind me.

I turned around and there she was. The old woman. She had rats sitting on her shoulders, rats gripping onto her clothes, and rats cupped in her hands.

"Vhat's de matter," she asked with a sly smile. "Aren't you de happiest girl on de earth? You certainly de tallest."

The rats all squealed their little rat giggles.

"Look what you did to me!" I yelled.

I picked her up off the floor, but she sunk her little pointy rat teeth into my hand! I dropped her back down.

"Don't you try to bully me, beeg girl!" she squeaked. "I gave you vhat you wanted! Now you so angry? You say you vant to be tall, I make you tall, eh?"

"But look at me!" I insisted. "I'm a freak! I'm a mutant. I can't even play anymore! I have no co-ordination. I've got no moves! I can't even control the ball! I'm a *giant*! Last practice, I shattered the entire backboard!"

"Aaaah. Just like de favorite player, eh? De Shakweel O'Neel, yes?"

"I don't want to be Shaquille O'Neal! I want to be Sarah Bardin! I want to *play ball* like *Sarah Bardin*!"

"Dat's not vhat you say before," she said, waving her finger at me.

"Well, that's what I'm saying now!" I yelled. "I want to be *me* again! There's got to be a way!

Isn't there some way to reverse the magic? To get rid of this curse? *Something?*"

"Sure there ees," she said simply.

"*What?*" I yelped. "There *is*? Why didn't you tell me?"

"You never ask," she squeaked. "I no see you coming to veesit de dirty leetle rats. Who vants to veesit de dirty leetle rats, eh?"

"I'm sorry! I'm sorry! Can you tell me what it is? Please! Tell me how to reverse the spell!"

"Eet's simple," she said. "De magic number. *Thirty-four stuffs make you tall enough, but thirty-four dribbles make you leetle!*"

"That's it?" I asked, grinning in disbelief. "I just have to dribble a ball thirty-four times and I'm me again?"

"In de game," the old woman whispered. "You must dribble de ball thirty-four times *in de game*. So . . . you vant to be small, you better get up de stairs, eh? Last game of de season, yes? You no do it in dees game, *you gonna get very, very big dis summer, eh*? You better get up there and dribble, dribble, *dribble! Hee-hee-hee-hee-squeeeak!*"

She started to laugh at me. Pretty soon, the entire basement of rats were laughing along with her.

Dribble the ball thirty-four times in the game! I could barely dribble at all!

Hee-hee-hee-hee-squeak-squeak-squeeeeeak!

I went back upstairs to the gym with a mission. I had to dribble that ball thirty-four times. I just had to. This was my last chance.

When I got back to the court, the second half had already started. The Tigers were winning the game.

"Sarah, where have you been?" Coach Jenkins asked, cocking her head to look up at me.

"I'm sorry, Coach. I had to do something. But I'm ready to go! Put me in the game."

"I'm going to sit you, Sarah," Coach Jenkins said. She didn't look happy about it.

"What?" I said, eyes bulging out of my head.

"Sarah," she said, "you're upsetting the parents. You're scaring the kids. You're even scaring me! And let's face it, you can't play ball."

Tears started rolling down my face. They plunked like raindrops on the coach's head.

"Coach," I cried. "You have to put me in the game! It's *very important* that I play in this game!"

"I'm sorry, Sarah," she said. "I can't do it.

Have a seat on the bench. You had a great season, but it's over. Now sit down."

"Coach," I pleaded. "You don't understand! It's a matter of life and death! If I don't play in this game . . . *we're all gonna be doomed!*"

"That's enough, Sarah!" she yelled. "*Sit down!*"

I stomped my foot down. The whole floor shook. The players all lost their balance on the court.

That's it, I thought to myself. I'm doomed. We're all doomed. By next week, I'll be stepping on my classmates, crushing buildings with my feet!

I couldn't fit in the folding chairs anymore. I dropped down on my backside, shaking the whole gym again. I held my giant knees in my giant arms and cried.

We kept our lead through the second half. Jeff was having a great game. I knew he was trying to play for the both of us.

But time was running out. There were only a few minutes left in the game. A few minutes left for my future as a normal human being! I couldn't let this happen. I had to do something! *I had to get in the game.*

I picked my huge body up off the court and stomped over to Coach Jenkins.

"Coach!" I shouted, looking down at her. "You have to put me in this game."

"I already told you, Sarah, you're out!" she said.

But that wouldn't do.

I reached down and picked Coach Jenkins up. We were face-to-face. And her feet were dangling in the air.

"Put . . . me . . . in . . . the . . . game," I said, almost growling.

Coach Jenkins knew I meant business.

"Yes, ma'am," she squeaked.

I bounded on the court and I grabbed the ball! As soon as I had it, I just started dribbling.

One, two, three, four, five, six—

One of the Washington Monuments stole the ball from me! He ran it downcourt and scored!

"Booooo!" the crowd started screaming. "Get the giant out of the game!"

Ignore them, Sarah. You've got to do this!

I took the ball on the inbound pass and started dribbling.

One, two, three, four, five, six, seven—

They stole the ball from me again mid-dribble! I was too huge! Each dribble was taking forever to bounce back up to my hand! It was *so easy* for this short girl on the Monuments to steal the ball away from me! They scored again! The Monuments were catching up and it was all my fault!

"*Booooo!*" screamed the crowd again. And again. And again. Every time I grabbed the ball, the crowd was booing, I was dribbling, and the Monuments were stealing the ball and scoring! They had actually taken the lead away from us! They were up by two.

"Get out of the game, you giant freak!" screamed Wendy. "You're gonna lose us the game! Coach! Take her out!"

Coach Jenkins just shook her head. She didn't have anything else to say.

The Tigers wouldn't pass me the ball anymore. I had to steal a pass from my own teammates just to get my hands on the ball. I started dribbling again.

"*Nooooo!*" screamed Wendy. "Stop standing there and dribbling! *Pass the ball, you freak!*"

"Sarah!" yelled Coach Jenkins. "You've got to bring the ball up court! Time is running out!"

Oh, no, I thought. Run and dribble at the same time?

I didn't think I could do it. But I had to try.

There were only ten seconds left in the game!

I started trying to move up court and dribble. I had my head hunched over, keeping my eyes on my dribble as I lumbered across the court.

The crowd was screaming its boos. I felt like I was moving in slow motion.

I was starting to get dizzy. I couldn't even see what was in front of me. And all I could hear . . . was squeaking. Squeaking coming from all around me.

The sneakers on the court all looked like little white rats scurrying all over. Every one of them squeaking, *squeaking*!

It was happening again! *While I was trying to dribble!*

"Nooooo!" I screamed. "Not now!"

My skin started rippling and stretching! It seemed like there were rats all over the court! Rats running around inside of me! My dribbling hand had something huge running around inside of it!

Squeeeeeak, squeak-squeak, squeeeeeak!

I was growing faster than I ever had before. Stretching up, up . . . straight toward the gym ceiling! From this height, all the players looked like rats, darting all around the court.

One of the little rats on the court started

running at me. She was the little Washington Monument who'd just stolen the ball from me. And she was going for the steal again.

"Nooooo!" I screamed down to her. *"Don't do it!"*

I was getting dizzier! I didn't know what to do. I had to finish this dribble! She came right at me.

But she missed the ball completely. She ran right into my leg!

"Whoa! Whooooaaaa!" I screamed. I had tripped on the little girl!

I was coming down.

"Look out!" screamed Wendy.

"Ahhhhh!" screamed the crowd.

Booooom!

The whole gym shook as I hit the floor.

Then I heard the whistle blow.

"That's a tripping foul!" shouted the ref.

I'd been fouled. I was going to the line.

CHAPTER
THIRTEEN

I stood at the foul line, staring down at the basket. My sweat was raining down all over my opponents. The crowd's boos were getting louder and louder.

But I didn't care.

Because I was standing behind the foul line. The one place where I could dribble as much as I wanted! Without anyone to stop me! And that's just what I was doing. Dribbling.

Every dribble was pounding down on the court.

We were still down by two, with ten seconds left.

"*Booooo!*" they shouted. "Stop dribbling the ball, and *shoot* it! *Booooo!*"

But on the thirty-fourth dribble, no one made a sound.

Overhead, the lights started flashing on and off. And a howling wind came sweeping through the whole gymnasium.

The crowd was getting blown flat against the bleachers! The kids on the court were trying to keep their balance as the wind threw them left and right. The cheerleaders were crashing into each other!

My whole body was bubbling and shaking.

But it was shrinking! It was definitely shrinking!

And something else was happening to me. Something *really* strange!

I was breathing out a sort of mist. There was black smoke coming out of my mouth and my nose! And you're not going to believe this, but the smoke was *laughing*!

Hee-hee-hee-hee-squeak-squeak-squeeeeeak!

The black smoke was flying around in the wind, squeaking and laughing at the crowd!

The smoke gathered itself in a big cloud and landed on the court right in front of me. And when it landed, *it was not just a cloud of smoke.* It looked more like little black balls of dust. And those little black dust balls were *alive.* They scurried around in front of me, squeaking and squealing.

And then they scurried off, squealing all the way. Soon they had disappeared.

The wind stopped. The lights were back to normal. *I* was back to normal.

The crowd was completely silent.

That was just fine with me. I like quiet when I'm shooting foul shots. And I made them both!

But the crowd was still stunned. They weren't speaking. They weren't moving. They were just staring at me.

"Hey!" I screamed to the entire gym. "I know you've never seen a giant turn into a dwarf, but the dwarf has just tied the score with ten seconds left in the game! *So let's make some noise!*"

The crowd was silent for a second. But then . . .

"Yeeeaaaaah!"

They started cheering like crazy!

"Let's go Tigers! Let's go Tigers!"

The Monuments had the ball. They passed it in to one of their tallest players. She was starting to dribble the ball up court.

But if there was one thing I'd learned, it was this: *A dwarf can steal that ball from a giant.*

I ducked inside and grabbed the ball away from her, right in the middle of her dribble!

The crowd was counting down the remaining seconds.

"Seven . . . six . . . five . . ."

I had the ball with five seconds left. I had to score. I had to get it in the hoop. It was up to me.

And suddenly it hit me! What the old woman had said to me in the basement about her little squeaking friends. *They could go places no one else could go. They could find de holes. Use de speed.* And I saw the hole! Right there in front of me. Between all those tall bodies. There was a lane. I just had to drive the lane!

The Monuments were converging on me, waving their hands all over the place! But I had seen the hole and I was going for it.

I dribbled back between my legs, shaking off the man to my right. I flipped the dribble to my right hand and drove the lane hard! I flew right between two huge players before they even knew where I was! A quick leap and a quick flick of the wrist . . . and the ball bounced right through the hoop.

The buzzer sounded.

"Yeeeaaaaah!" The crowd went insane!

We had done it! The Tigers had won the championship!

The entire crowd stormed the court. There were people everywhere! I started running through the crowd, looking for Jeff.

Instead, I ran right into the old woman.

She was smiling.

"I knew you could do eet! Leetle girl hits beeg shot, eh?"

"You were right!" I yelled. "Everything you said!"

"Of course I was right!"

"But did you have to make it so *awful*?" I yelled.

"Leetle girl needed *beeg* lesson!" she announced.

I had to admit, it made sense.

"Do you want to come celebrate with us?" I asked. "You can bring your little friends!"

"I cannot stay," she explained. "There is a leetle boy at de Abraham Leencoln School. He theenks he vants to be *older*! My leetle friends and I, we going to teach him a leetle lesson, eh?"

"Poor kid," I said.

"Is there anytheeng else we can do for *you*?"

I thought about it for a second.

"Actually," I said with a sly smile, "you see that girl standing over there?"

I was pointing at Wendy.

"Ahhh," said the old woman. "De beeg bully, eh?"

"That's right," I said.

"Maybe my friends and I should say a leetle *'hello,'* yes?"

"Yes," I said, grinning from ear to ear.

"*Noooo problem.* Good-bye, leetle girl. Be happy, eh?"

"I will be," I said. "Thank you."

And then she was gone.

Next thing I saw was Wendy screaming.

"Ahhhhh! *Rats!* There are rats in this gym! Help me! *Heeeeelp meeeee!*"

They chased her out of the gym.

Jeff finally found me in the crowd. He gave me a huge high five and started hollering at the top of his lungs.

"You did it! I knew you could do it, Sarah! Wooooo!"

He was about to lift me onto his shoulders, but I stopped him.

"*Don't pick me up!*" I screamed. "I like it right where I am!"